PETER IN BLUEBERRY LAND

Elsa Beskow

Floris Books

PETER IN BLUEBERRY LAND

Elsa Beskow

Floris Books

First published in 1901 in Swedish under the title
Puttas Äventyr i Blåbärsskogen by Albert Bonniers, Stockholm
First published in English in 1982 by Ernest Benn Ltd
Tenth impression published in 2001 by Floris Books
15 Harrison Gardens, Edinburgh
© 2001 BonniersCarlsen Förlag
English version by Alison Sage © Ernest Benn Ltd, 1982
British Library CIP Data available
ISBN 0-86315-050-0
Printed in Belgium

Early one morning, Peter went into the forest. He was carrying two baskets; one for red cranberries and one for blue blueberries. It was his mother's birthday and they were going to be a surprise present for her. But where *were* the berries?

Peter could not find a single berry. Deeper and deeper he went into the forest, until at last he sat down on a tree stump and burst into tears.

Suddenly, he felt a light tap on his shoe. "Cheer up, Peter," said a voice. There was a tiny old man, no bigger than an apple. "I'm the King of Blueberry Land and I'll show you where they grow."

Peter was so surprised he didn't know what to say. A second time the old man tapped him lightly on the shoe with his tiny blue wand — and Peter was as small as he was! The heather seemed to grow in great bushes, the grasses tall as spears and the wild flowers were as big as crowns.

Peter's baskets were now much too big for him to carry and so the blueberry king whistled up two squirrels. In a flash, they swung the baskets onto their backs and bounded away.

Soon they were walking under ferns like huge palm trees and Peter could hardly believe how different and interesting it all looked. There was an acorn, big as a helmet — and there was a spider. Peter was not sure if he was glad to see him, although the spider tried to look friendly.

"Here we are," said the blueberry king cheerfully, when they reached a little wood full of fruit trees.

"Look!" said Peter excitedly. "Blue apples!"

"Don't be silly," said the king, laughing. "They're blueberries. But come and meet my sons."

Seven boys were playing ball with the berries and they came running up to meet Peter. Their clothes were splashed with the dark blue juice.

' Peter has come looking for blueberries," said the king. "Let's see how quickly we can fill his basket."

The boys scrambled up the trees, laughing and tasting the ripe berries as they tossed them down. Peter tasted some of the berries too.

As soon as his basket was filled to the brim, the boys gathered round him shouting, ''Now it's time to play. Come on, Peter!''

They let Peter steer their bark boat as they slipped though the cool, green water, past dragonflies and lilypads, their leaf sail swelling gently in the breeze. Peter forgot all about berry-picking until one of his new friends said, ''We'll be late for Mrs Cranberry. She's waiting for us with some fruit for you. Hurry up, Peter!''

Quickly, they beached their boat. They combed their hair, cleaned their teeth and washed their hands which were still blue with the sticky juice.

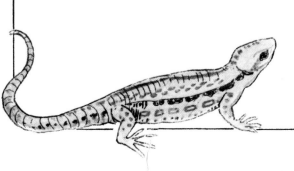

Eight brown mice were
waiting for them under the
blueberry trees. Away they
galloped, through sunlight and
shade, over the springy thyme
and sweet moss. Peter had
hardly time to catch his breath,
when they reached a little
clearing. In the middle was a
cottage made of cranberry twigs.

Outside in the sun sat
Mrs Cranberry and her five
daughters, polishing berries.
The shiniest and reddest fruit
they put in a pot to cook with
honey.

"Peter!" shouted the girls, when they saw him.

"Mind you pick those berries carefully," warned Mrs Cranberry, who could be sharp at times; but the girls were already gathering the fruit. Two curious ladybirds came to watch, so the girls sang, *ladybird, ladybird, fly away home* to them.

When Peter's basket was as
full as it could be, they all had
time to play. They took turns on
the spider's web swing and when
a cricket started up a song, three
of the girls joined in the chorus.

Then Mrs Cranberry rang the dinner bell, and all sorts of other guests, yellow butterflies, ants and bees, hurried back with the children. Everyone ate the delicious juicy red cranberries and honey until they were full. Peter could only manage two.

But now it was time to go and Peter said ''thank you'' to Mrs Cranberry and goodbye to her daughters. His basket was now so full that everyone had to load it onto a wagon. Then they harnessed the mice and away they flew, although not as fast as before.

They raced past two snails, who went green with envy, wishing they could travel so fast. The blueberry king was waiting for them when they arrived home. ''Take Peter back to where we first met,'' he ordered the mice.

''Oh, don't go yet!'' cried the blueberry boys and Peter begged their father to let him stay for just one more game. The king smiled and shook his head.

''It's getting late and your mother will be worried. Perhaps you will come and visit us another day.'' ''Goodbye!'' shouted everyone, as Peter climbed into the wagon again. ''Come back soon!''

Suddenly, Peter stopped with a jerk. He was back on his tree stump and there was no sign of the blueberry king, or his sons, or even the whisker of one of his mice.

"I must have been dreaming," said Peter to himself. He looked down, and there at his feet were two baskets, both neatly filled; one with cranberries and one with blueberries. So it had all been true!

When he got home, he drew a birthday card for his mother. (His big sister Kate helped him a little with the spelling.) Here it is. He picked these flowers for his mother too, and put them round the baskets of berries.

His mother was very pleased and said it was one of the nicest presents she had ever had. "Where did you find all those berries?" she asked. But Peter smiled and shook his head. It was a secret between him and the King of Blueberry Land.